SNOOPY, COME HOME

A NEW *PEANUTS* BOOK

by Charles M. Schulz

HOLT, RINEHART AND WINSTON

New York · Chicago · San Francisco

In Canada, Holt, Rinehart
and Winston of Canada, Limited.

Library of Congress Catalog Card Number: 63-10087

Published, February, 1963
Eleventh Printing, June, 1969

SBN: 03–031160–8

Printed in the United States of America

SNOOPY,
COME HOME

Books by Charles M. Schulz

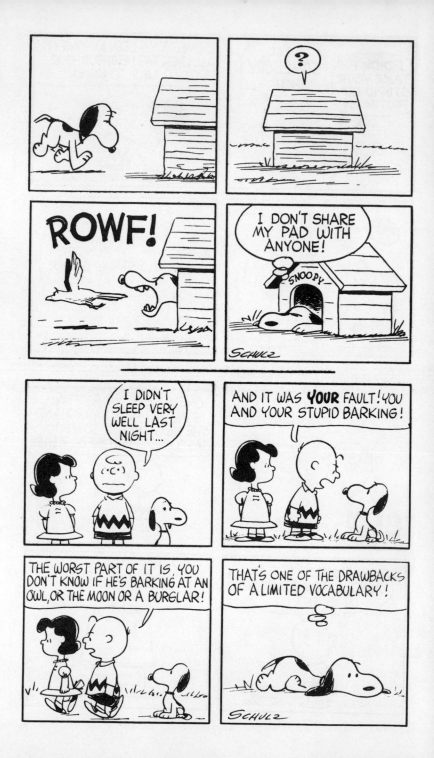

WHENEVER A SHOW COMES ON ABOUT HUNTING, **I** LEAVE!

ARF ARF ARF ARF

"BARKING DOGS NEVER BITE"

WHY DO YOU SUPPOSE THAT IS, CHARLIE BROWN?

I DON'T KNOW... MAYBE IT'S JUST A SAYING...

NO, IT'S BECAUSE IT'S A REAL GOOD WAY TO BITE YOUR TONGUE!

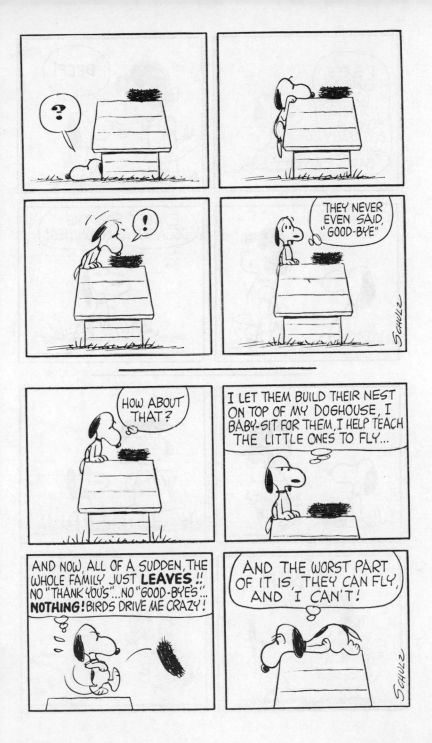